W9-CBZ-026

I Don't Want to Talk About It

by

Jeanie Franz Ransom

illustrated by

Kathryn Kunz Finney

MAGINATION PRESS

WASHINGTON, DC

Amazon 12/05
$8.95

For Rebecca Jean — J.F.R.

For Madison — K.K.F.

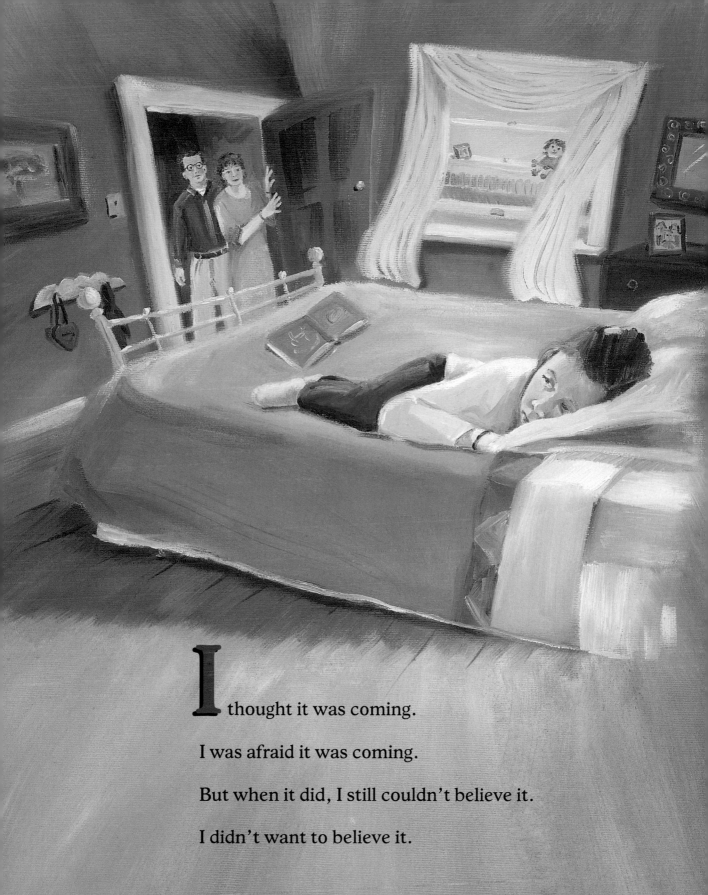

I thought it was coming.

I was afraid it was coming.

But when it did, I still couldn't believe it.

I didn't want to believe it.

"We need to talk to you about something," my father said.

He and my mother sat down across from each other like two birds on a telephone wire, with me in the middle. I just kept reading my book, trying not to hear, wanting not to hear.

My mother placed her hand gently alongside my face, like she does when I've had a bad dream. I wished *this* was a dream.

"Your father and I are getting a divorce," she said. I wanted to pull my whole body inside a shell like a turtle, so that my mother's words couldn't hurt me. Especially that one word: divorce.

"You've probably noticed that your mother and I haven't been getting along very well," my father said.

"We tried very hard to work out our differences," my mother said quietly, "but we weren't able to."

I remembered the nights I wanted to be an elephant, so that I could crash through my parents' door and stop their mad, bad words.

"I don't want to talk about it," I said.

"It must be hard to hear us tell you this," my mother said.

"Talking about it might help." She ran her fingers through my hair, like she always does when I feel sad or upset.

"I don't want to talk about it," I said.

I wanted to toss my mane and run away like a wild horse, run as fast as the wind, as far as I could go.

"You're probably going to have lots of different feelings," my mother said. "Most kids do when this happens to them."

"I don't want to talk about it," I said.

I wanted to be prickly like a porcupine, so that I couldn't be hurt by anything or anybody anymore.

"It's okay to feel mad," my father said.

"I don't want to talk about it," I said.

I wanted to be a crocodile and gobble both my parents and their terrible, horrible news right up.

"It's okay to feel sad, too," my mother said.

"I don't want to talk about it," I said.

I wanted to be a fish, so that my tears

could fall into the river and no one would know

how much I wanted to cry.

"It's okay to feel scared," my father said.

"I don't want to talk about it," I said. I wanted to be a lion with a roar so loud that everyone would think I was very brave.

"None of this is your fault," my father said. "It's a grown-up problem, just between your mom and me."

"Your dad and I have had a lot of disagreements lately," my mother said. "But one thing we never disagree about is how wonderful you are and how much we love you."

"I DON'T WANT TO TALK ABOUT IT!" I shouted.

The room got very quiet.

My mom reached out her arms.

I moved a little bit closer. My dad did, too.

"I want to be a baby kangaroo and ride in your pocket,"
I said to them.

"That way, we couldn't leave you," my mom said.

I nodded. She understood.

"I will always be your mom.

Dad will always be your dad," she said.

"And we will *never* leave you."

I pushed away from my mother's arms and rolled off the bed.

I pretended to look out the window. It was spring.

The robins were flying back from their winter homes.

"Talking about it might help," my mom said.

I saw a bird hopping around our backyard, searching for something.

"I'd like to be that robin and fly away from all of you!" I cried.

My dad said gently, "Mom and I would fly after you and bring you home."

My mom and dad came over to the window, and stood next to me. We watched the robin inspect the birdhouse my dad and I made last year.

"Where am I going to live?" I wondered out loud.

"You'll live with me part of the time, and part of the time with Dad," said my mom. "We'll work it out so that you'll be spending time with both of us every week."

"We'll see each other a lot," said my dad, "and you can talk to Mom or me on the phone whenever you want."

"When I'm with you, will we still cook and play checkers

and go to the movies, like always?" I asked my dad.

"That won't change," said my dad.

"And when I'm with you, will we still garden and read and go on walks, like always?" I asked my mom.

"That won't change, either," said my mom.

So much had changed so fast. I was glad to hear that *some* things would stay the same.

My dad said, "We'll be living in different houses, but I think they'll be happier houses."

I hoped so.

"So I guess I'll be kind of like the robin, with two places to live."

"Kind of," my mom said. "And you'll be loved wherever you are."

I reached out and gave Mom and Dad a little bear hug.

And got a big bear hug right back.

Note to Parents

by Philip Stahl, Ph.D.

Divorce is almost always traumatic for children. However, with careful planning and good communication, parents can reduce its negative effects and help their children adjust to the changes in ways that are healthy and positive. As a separated or divorced parent, the most valuable steps you can take to accomplish this are:

- encourage open communication, allowing your child to ask questions and helping him or her to express feelings fully and appropriately;
- as much as possible, preserve the continuity of the relationship between the child and each parent, so that both parents remain involved in the child's academic, social, extracurricular, and emotional lives;
- provide a consistent and healthy daily routine in the child's home or homes, regardless of the parenting schedule that has been set up;
- be supportive and positive regarding the other parent.

Expect your child to experience many feelings. These may include:

- guilt (they may think they were responsible for the divorce or didn't do enough to prevent it; they may feel guilty about feeling relieved if the parental conflict is substantially reduced after the divorce decision),
- sadness (they miss the family structure and want you back together),
- loneliness (they may withdraw from others to hide their feelings),
- anger (they are mad that you have disrupted the family structure),
- confusion (they don't know what to expect and, possibly, what to believe; they don't understand some or any of their possibly conflicting feelings),
- fear (they wonder such things as: Will my parents leave me like they left each other? Will they stop loving me like they stopped loving each other? Will I have to move? Will I never get to see one of my parents again? Will I still get to take piano lessons?).

In the midst of these emotions, your child's understanding of them may be limited as he or she expresses them in a variety of ways. Some children may exhibit small regressions, such as toileting accidents, playing with toys meant for younger children, or use of immature language. Your child may seem unusually quiet, anxious, sad, irritable, or forgetful. His performance at school may slip. He may lose interest in sports or other activities that he once enjoyed. He may no longer want to play with friends. He may try to act like a perfect child to ensure your love for him or mend what he thinks might be the problem in the family.

Because young children often don't know exactly what they are feeling or why, it can be difficult for them to talk about the sadness, fear, anger, and confusion that most children of divorcing parents experience. In addition, children may not want to talk about their feelings, because they fear they will further destabilize an already unsteady situation. This is especially so when they are feeling angry. Children may fear that talking will release the anger, which will rage out of control and blow up what remains of their world. Finally, many young children fear that merely thinking or talking about a bad thing can make the bad thing come true.

Despite these challenges, parents can help their children recognize and deal with their feelings in ways that are comforting and effective. The parents in this story are good role models in terms of showing what to tell a child and how to say it. For example, whenever possible, it is best that both parents begin by talking to their children together about the decision to divorce. Appearing together is reassuring, in that it demonstrates that you will continue to work together on their behalf, even though your marriage is ending. Also, it is helpful for your child to hear that most kids in this situation have lots of feelings, and by naming the feelings you validate them for your child. You can use *I Don't Want to Talk About It* to introduce some of the feelings—including the desire not to talk about them!

Respond actively to your child's nonverbal expressions as they occur. If you see your child crying, give her a hug, tell her it's good to cry when she's feeling sad, and let her know that most children do feel sad when their parents divorce. If she refuses to participate in the Little League games that she once loved, be gentle but firm that she continue with the activity, saying something like, "I know that you don't feel like going right now, but I can almost promise you that you'll feel much better about it once you are there, and that you'll be glad that you went. It's really important that we keep doing the things we love and that make us happy." If she is irritable for no obvious reason, you might say in a comforting voice, "Something seems to be bothering you. Would you like to talk about it? Maybe I can help."

Suggest without pressure that talking *does* help, and repeat this suggestion from time to time so that your child knows there is no "statute of limitations." Over the first few weeks, in particular, talk with him individually and together many times to be sure that he understands what divorce is and what it is not, and to reassure him of your ongoing love and availability. Certain things should be said to young children even when they don't ask. One, tell your child that talking about bad feelings doesn't make bad things happen. Two, tell him that you will always love him and be his mom or dad, and that divorce doesn't change that. And three, reassure him that divorce is a grown-up problem, and that he had nothing to do with why it is happening in your family.

Along those lines, a child of divorced parents does best when her parents avoid exposing her to conflict between the two of them. Working to make the exchanges between you and the other parent child-focused and peaceful, speaking respectfully of each other, and resisting competition with each other will go a long way toward helping your child adjust—and ultimately, your own life will be easier, too. Also, these efforts will have a lasting, positive effect on your relationship with your child, and possibly on your child's future relationships with others as well.

A predictable schedule and regular routines will help your child feel more secure and more in control of parts of her life. Not only does a schedule permit her to know where she will be from day to day, allowing her—and you—to conduct school, social, and other plans, but it also offers the steady reassurance of spending time with both parents. Keep in mind that children between the ages of 4 and 8 are quite concrete in their thinking. Their sense of abstractions such as time is not yet at the same level as the older child's, so they may not understand ideas like "every other day" or "every other weekend." When you talk with them about the family schedule, use calendars with colors or letters to designate where they will be and when.

Along with maintaining a predictable schedule, maintain the same rules and expectations you had before the divorce—and resist relaxing them out of guilt feelings on your part. Occasionally children "act out" their anger or distress by fighting with peers or siblings, avoiding school work, or otherwise misbehaving. Use these moments as opportunities to reinforce limits and to help your child find healthy ways to express and cope with his feelings. You might say, for example, "You can't hit your sister, but there are other things you can do when you are angry. Let's think of some better ways to get out your angry feelings." Also, give a child positive attention when he's expressing himself appropriately so that he doesn't need to get in trouble to get your attention.

The more you can minimize changes that result from your divorce, the better your child will be able to cope with the changes that are required. Familiar settings and things provide an anchor of security, just as predictable rules and routines do. Encourage your child to take important objects between homes, and focus on solutions rather than blame when needed items are inevitably forgotten. Remember, your child's special things should be with your child, and when children are this young it is the parents' job to make sure that teddy bears, schoolwork, and athletic equipment are there when needed.

Try using your own feelings as a guide to understanding and addressing your child's. For example, you might say to her, "You seem more withdrawn than you used to be. Are you afraid of anything? I know that when I'm afraid, I sometimes like to be by myself, but I've learned that talking about my feelings helps me feel better." At the same time, while it may be helpful to your children to hear you talk about your own feelings in general terms, remember that children are not prepared to handle your emotional reactions to the stresses associated with divorce. This could lead to their feeling guilty or responsible for taking care of your feelings. Younger children are most susceptible to this. Find and use adult supports for discussions about the details of your struggles, so that your children are free to focus on their own feelings and reactions.

Your child may feel like talking about what's on his mind at unexpected moments, such as when you are in the car alone together, while you're making dinner, or while you're playing a board game. Be available to listen and respond. If he chooses a time when you are truly unable to give your full attention, tell him that you really want to talk and specify when you'll be able to, then follow up. Even if he is no longer in a frame of mind to open up, he will get the important message that you care and that he can talk to you when he is ready.

Make open communication a habit by talking with your children about the divorce and your family on a regular basis over the coming years. As they get older—ages 10, 13, 16—they will continue to have questions as their concerns change and evolve.

Philip Stahl, Ph.D., is a psychologist with a private practice specializing in divorce and custody issues. He is also a national expert in the field of custody evaluation, and the author of several books, including Parenting After Divorce *(Impact, 2000). Dr. Stahl lives in Northern California.*

Published by
MAGINATION PRESS
An Educational Publishing Foundation Book
American Psychological Association
750 First Street, NE
Washington, DC 20002

For more information about our books, including a complete catalog, please write to us, call 1-800-374-2721, or visit our website at: www.maginationpress.com

The text type is Stratford.
Editor: Darcie Conner Johnston
Art Director: Susan K. White

Library of Congress Cataloging-in-Publication Data

Ransom, Jeanie Franz, 1957-
I don't want to talk about it / written by Jeanie Franz Ransom ;
afterword by Philip Stahl ; illustrated by Kathryn Kunz Finney.
p. cm.
Summary: After reluctantly talking with her parents about their upcoming divorce, a young girl discovers that there will be some big changes but that their love for her will remain the same. Includes an afterword for parents on helping children through such a change.
ISBN 1-55798-664-9 (hard) — ISBN 1-55798-703-3 (soft)
[1. Divorce—Fiction.] I. Finney, Kathryn Kunz, 1960- ill. II. Title.

PZ7.R1744 Id 2000
[E]—dc21   00-027036

Printed in China

10 9 8 7 6 5